Daisy's in Bloom

Written and Illustrated by
Lisa A. LeFrois-Heath

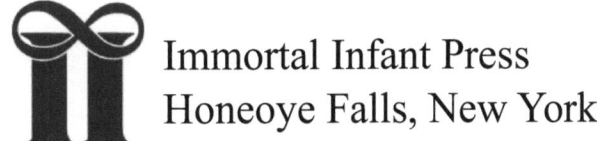
Immortal Infant Press
Honeoye Falls, New York

Library of Congress Control Number: 9780988959613

ISBN: 978-0-9889596-1-3

For additional information, please contact:
www.lalefroisheath.com
info@lalefroisheath.com

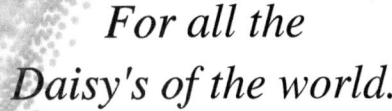

For all the
Daisy's of the world.

Special thanks to:

Jim and Emily,
for your continued
patience, love, and support.

Dr. Megan Norcia,
The College at Brockport,
State University of New York.

This book is dedicated to
every misfit, outcast, geek, nerd, and freak
who's ever felt like they don't belong.

In the immortal words of John Lennon,
"We all shine on..."

Daisy's foot landed gently on the sidewalk as she slowly stepped off the school bus. The sound of children laughing in the distance filled the air as she quietly gained her balance. Daisy knew all the kids were excited because her bus was the last bus of the day to arrive at Miss Judy's house. But she also knew none of the kids were waiting to see *her*. They were just happy because today was Friday.

You see, Friday was the last day of the school week and instead of doing homework, Miss Judy let them play flag football outside. *Everyone* looked forward to Friday's. Everyone, that is, except Daisy. In fact, Daisy had been dreading Friday all week long and she felt nervous and a little wobbly as Miss Judy reached for her hand. After all, it had only been a few months since the accident. Daisy hadn't really had much time to get used to her new leg yet. And the thought of playing flag football? Well...it made her stomach do flip-flops inside.

Miss Judy held Daisy's hand as they crossed the street and for a moment, Daisy pretended she was holding her mother's hand. It was soft and gentle and it made her feel warm inside. But it just wasn't the same. Daisy missed her mother's touch and she began to feel sad.

"I'm okay...I'm fine, really," Daisy told Miss Judy as she steadied herself on the sidewalk. When she was ready, they walked into the backyard where all the kids were waiting.

There they were. All eight of them. Laughing and joking without a care in the world. But as soon as they saw Daisy coming, it got real quiet and whispers filled the air. Daisy could feel them all staring at her and she wanted to runaway and hide.

"Okay, it's time to pick teams!" announced Miss Judy.

"Oh, great...here we go..." thought Daisy. She wanted to ask Miss Judy why she even had to play in the first place? After all, there were already an even number of kids for each team. Daisy wondered what they even needed her for anyway?

Suddenly, Jack broke the silence and when he spoke up, it was if he had been reading Daisy's mind.

"Not for nothin, Miss Judy, but how's Daisy gonna run on that leg o' hers anyways?"

"Now Jack," Miss Judy said sternly. "What kinda thing is that to say?"

"Well, I'm sorry, Maam. But I been lookin' forward to this game all week. And we don't need no one who can't run, or someone we gotta be careful of. We wanna win, and she ain't gonna do nothin' but hold us all back."

Daisy felt her cheeks burning, she was hot all over, and her face turned bright red as tears welled up inside of her. She didn't *want* to cry in front of everyone, especially Jack, but she just couldn't help it.

"Oh, Dear!" Miss Judy cried, as she waved her hands in the air and placed her arm around Daisy's shoulder.

"I'm so sorry, Daisy! Jack doesn't know what he's saying!"

"Oh, yes he does! Just leave me alone!" Daisy shouted as she pushed Miss Judy away from her. "Just leave me alone!"

Tears were flowing steadily from Daisy's eyes now, and when she looked around at everyone, she felt a million eyes staring right back at her.

"They hate me," she thought to herself. "They hate me, and I don't blame them! Look at me! I'm broken...I'm damaged...I can't do anything. I'm useless!"

At that moment, all Daisy could think about was running away. But how? How could she ever run again? The doctors *said* her new leg could do all the same things her old one could, the way it did before she lost it in the accident. But she didn't believe them and she'd never even tried. And at that particular moment, she didn't even care anymore. All she wanted was her old life back. To get off the bus at her own house, just like she used to before coming to Miss Judy's. She wanted to do cartwheels up the driveway while her mother smiled and waited for her at the front door. But now, she thought, "I'll *never* see my mom again, and I'll *never* do cartwheels again. **Never!"**

Daisy stood motionless, sobbing in front of everyone for what felt like forever. And when she just couldn't take it anymore, she turned toward the woods at the edge of Miss Judy's yard. Instantly and without thinking too much about it, she steadied her foot firmly on the ground in front of her and pushed off on her metal leg. It felt awkward at first and she worried the other kids were still watching her and laughing. But she decided she didn't care anymore because she had to run away...and *fast!*

To Daisy's surprise, when her metal foot touched the ground, she felt it spring back and as she brought it forward and pushed off again, she instantly felt a jolt of power beneath her.

12

Daisy was amazed at her newfound strength and broke into a light jog as she headed toward the woods. Even though tears were still streaming down her face, she started to feel good as she pumped her fists and put one foot in front of the other, moving faster and faster with each passing stride. Daisy ran and ran for what seemed like hours and when she couldn't run anymore, she simply fell to the ground and landed on a soft bed of pine needles. The dusky, golden rays of the sun peeked through the tree tops and warmed the earth as she fell fast asleep, cradled beneath the magic of the woods.

This is **the** most beautiful place I've ever seen! But where am I, and how did I get here?

Daisy wiped stardust from her eyes as she heard the sound of birds chirping and the soft whisper of the wind echoing in her ear. She sat up to find a beautiful pond stretched out before her glistening like a million sapphires glowing in the sun. Fresh dew shone like diamonds on the tree tops and the willowy edges of the grass sparkled like emeralds. Daisy was in awe of the beauty surrounding her and gasped in delight as she took in a breath of cool, fresh morning air. And then suddenly, it dawned on her. "I have no idea where I am, or how I got here?"

So...
whadda ya think
of me now, Jack?
Wanna race?
Bring it!

Just then, Daisy felt a strange ache in the upper part of her leg. As she massaged her thigh, she looked down at the ice blue, cold piece of steel attached to it.

Suddenly, memories of the accident, her mother's funeral, the loss of her leg, and of course, the game of flag at Miss Judy's...and Jack...all came flooding back to her. Daisy started to feel sad again, but then she remembered the way she took off running and couldn't help but wonder *what* Jack thought of her *now?* A faint smile crossed her lips.

Daisy closed her eyes for a moment and tried to imagine the look on Jack's face when she felt a gust of wind brush against her cheek. When she opened her eyes, she could barely believe what she saw standing in the grass before her! It was the most beautiful, breathtaking flower she'd ever seen! It had six petals, each a different color, all shiny and sparkling bright in the sun. It was amazing, and Daisy never imagined anything like this existed anywhere in the world!

"Oh, my," she shreiked. "It's magnificant!"

Daisy just had to get a better look at it. But each time she took a step closer, the wind grew stronger and stronger, until at last she was upon the flower.

The wind picked up and Daisy gazed in awe as the flower began spinning around and around, growing bigger and bigger with each passing turn. The faster it spun, the brighter it got and before long, it had spun itself into a huge, twirling ball of rainbow colors and it's center shone just like the sun! In fact, the heart of the flower was *so* bright, when Daisy gazed upon it she saw her own reflection staring right back at her!

"Why, it's just like looking into a mirror!" she exclaimed. "But I look so *different*. I barely recognize myself. Is that really *me*?" she wondered.

As Daisy gazed deeper into her own eyes her body tingled all over, she felt light as a feather, and she was sure the flower was quite magical, indeed. Slowly, the wind died down and when, at last, it stopped and her reflection began to fade, Daisy blinked in disbelief and when she opened her eyes, the flower was gone.

17

Silence filled the air until the rumble of footsteps along the shoreline startled Daisy and she looked around in a fright.

"Hello? Hello? Is anybody there?" she asked, as the smell of lilacs filled the air.

"Well, *hellloooh*," a snide little voice answered back, and Daisy soon discovered the source of the commotion standing before her in the grass. It was a champagne colored pig with the smoothest, shiniest hide she'd ever seen! It had diamond necklaces draped around it's neck and pink ribbons tied on it's ears, all sparkly and glistening in the sun.

"Oh my goodness...you're quite a spectacle, aren't you?!" Daisy blurted out.

"Such manners! And just exactly who might *youuuu* be?" the pig asked, her snout tilted slightly toward the sky.

"Oh, I'm terribly sorry," Daisy stammered. "I didn't mean to offend you. I'm just very confused. My name is Daisy. I have no idea where I am, and I just saw this flower...well, nevermind. You probably wouldn't believe me anyway."

"Probably not, but if you *must* know, this is Crystal Pond. My name's Kaela, and if you *don't* mind, it's time for my morning *baaath*."

"Bath? What do you mean bath?" Daisy chuckled. "Pigs don't take baths!"

"Well, hmmph," Kaela snorted. "*I'm* no ordinary pig, you see."

At that, Kaela jumped off the bank and did a belly flop right across the water. She splashed around a bit before coming ashore, spraying Daisy with warm pond water as she shook herself off.

"Now, if you'll excuse me for just a moment, I need to get something...right...over...here." Kaela reached behind Daisy to find a bottle of perfume hidden under a nearby leaf.

"Is *that* what I smell?!" Daisy wondered, crinkling her nose.

"Well, *excuuuse* me! Does my scent *offend* you?" Kaela snorted again, spraying herself generously.

"Ahem, ahem," Daisy coughed. "I'm sorry. Once again, please excuse me. Where I come from, pigs don't bathe, have soft, shiny skin, or wear beautiful jewelry and ribbons. They pretty much just hang out in dirty pig pens all day long, snorting and rolling around in the mud."

"Oh, that's what *everyone* thinks and it's quite *dreary, really*. But I guess I should be used to it by now. Like I said, *I'm* no ordinary pig. I *used* to like playing in the dirt when I was a piglet. But then one day, the farmer's daughter, Ella, wanted to play 'princess' with me. She bathed me in lilac water, dressed me in a fancy golden gown, tied ribbons in my ears, painted my hooves, and pushed me around the farm in a baby stroller while all the other pigs looked on in horror. It was *dreadfully* embarassing, to say the least!"

"Oh, that sounds awful!"

"I was simply *mortified*!" Kaela continued. "And if *that* wasn't bad enough, when it was time to go back in the pen, none of the other pigs would talk to me and they laughed at me behind my back, *all* the time."

"So, whatever did you do?" Daisy asked.

"Well, I did the only thing a self-respecting pig could do. I broke out of the pen one night and rolled away! I rolled over hills, along hedgerows and through the woods, until I stumbled here, upon Crystal Pond."

"Then you must have seen the flower, too?"

"Well...maybe I have, and maybe I have *not*."

"Huh?" Daisy wondered. "What's that supposed to mean?" Just then, a light breeze swept through Daisy's hair, she closed her eyes, and when she looked upon the pond again, Kaela was gone.

Daisy sat confused on the banks of Crystal Pond, wondering *what* Kaela meant when she said, 'maybe I have, and maybe I have *not?*'"

"Well, at least *now* I know where I am," she thought outloud. "Crystal Pond. It's such a *beautiful* place, but everything here is *sooo* different. The flower, the pig. What exactly *is* this place?"

"Ohhh, Crystal Pond is *many* things," an unfamiliar, but excited voice answered.

"Ummm...who said that?" Daisy wondered, ducking down low as a bat suddenly swooshed by overhead.

"Crystal Pond is a place where everything is and isn't," the bat spoke frantically. "All things here used to be something else, yet nothing here is what it's supposed to be. *My* name is Zara. Pleased to make your acquaintance."

"Ummm. Hi...I'm Daisy. It's nice to meet you, too. But I have no idea what you just said? I'm very confused. I saw this flower, I met this pig. Oh, what's the use? You probably wouldn't believe me anyway."

"What...what makes you say that?"

Zara was fluttering quickly now in front of Daisy, who was trying to get a good look at her wings. They were quite magnificant, all silver and shimmery in the sunlight. Daisy thought all bats had black wings and beady, brown eyes as well. But Zara had big, wide, twinkling blue eyes that seemed to reflect everything in the world around her.

"A bat with blue eyes? Now how can *that* be? *Unless...*," Daisy asked, "Zara? Zara...can you *see* me?"

"Why, yes, Daisy...yes I can," Zara answered, as she batted her eyelashes quickly and flapped her wings, swaying from side to side.

"That's right! Zara's the name, and seein's my game!"

"But I thought *all* bats were supposed to be blind? But you...you're not blind at all?!"

"Umm...didn't we just cover that? No...I'm not blind, Daisy. But I *used* to be. In fact, I was actually born *blind as a bat*, same as the rest of the bats in my colony of origin. But then, one night when we were out flying, I got stuck in a loose electrical wire and it *zapped* me. I mean, it zapped me *good!* I got real nervous and my radar just stopped working. The next night when I went out flying with the other bats, I kept bumping into things and everyone started making fun of me. After a while, I had trouble sleeping during the day, I talked *all* the time, my wings wouldn't stop flapping, and I drove all the other bats crazy! And the cave...well, *the cave* just didn't agree with my delicate constitution anymore. I started getting sick alot, and then one day, it was so cold in there I couldn't sleep. So I went outside to get warm and to my surprise when I opened my eyes, I discovered I could see!! I mean, I could see *all* the beautiful colors of the world! The bluest skies, the brightest clouds, and the greenest trees! On that day, I decided I *never* wanted to go back inside that dark, dreary, *boring* cave again."

"So, whatever did you do?" Daisy asked.

"Well, I couldn't control myself and I just took off flying. I flew and flew until my wings felt like they were going to fall right off! That's when I fell to the ground and landed here, on Crystal Pond."

"Then *you* must have seen the flower, too?" Daisy wanted to know.

"Well...maybe I have, and maybe I have not."

"Oh, great! Here we go again," thought Daisy. "What's the big idea?" she asked. But Zara did not answer, and when Daisy looked up toward the sky, she was gone.

Daisy scratched her head and tried to make sense of the day. One thing was for sure. Here, on the banks of Crystal Pond, Daisy didn't feel like such a freak anymore and she began to think being different might not be *so* bad after all. Then, suddenly from out of nowhere, a black cloud appeared overhead casting a long dark shadow over the banks of the pond. Strangely, though, Daisy didn't feel the least bit scared. Rather, she felt a light, gentle touch on her shoulder that reminded her of her mother.

"Mom, is that you? Are you out there? It's me, Daisy!"

"Oh, no! I'm so sorry. I'm afraid it's just me, Daisy. My name is Aldora. Sorry about the whole dark cloud *thing*. I was just fanning my wing!"

Aldora was the most *beautiful* butterfly Daisy had ever seen. She had see-thru golden wings, and even though one of them was bent, they still glistened in the sun, like a million crystals lighting up the sky.

"Pleased to meet you, Aldora. But how did you know my name?"

"Why, I heard it echoing in the woods, dear. I got here as fast as I could," Aldora said, motioning with her head to her broken wing.

"Forgive me for asking, Aldora. But what happened to your wing?"

"Well, you see, once when I was a baby caterpillar, I climbed a strong, old oak tree in the forest and built a cocoon on a high branch. I'd hope to stay there until, well, you know...the big change. But one day, a group of loggers came through the forest and started cutting down trees. I tried to inch my way down, but I couldn't move fast enough before the branch fell crashing to the ground. My wing must have broken in the fall because when I metamorphosized, it came out bent, like this." Aldora motioned again to her strangely shaped wing.

"Soon, the migration came, and I tried to keep up with the other butterflies, but it was just no use," she continued.

"So, whatever did you do?" Daisy asked.

"Why, I did the only thing a butterfly with a broken wing could do, dear. I started walking and before I knew it, I walked right out of the forest. In fact, I traveled so far both my legs collapsed beneath my wings and I fell fast asleep. When I woke up I found myself here, on the banks of Crystal Pond."

"So, then, you can't fly at all and you walk everywhere?"

"Well sort of. I mean, I can't *literally* spread both my wings and fly. But that doesn't mean I can't soar through the air just the same!"

"Forgive me, Aldora. But I don't understand how you can fly without *both* wings, and I'm afraid I just don't understand this place at all."

"Oh, it's really quite simple, dear. I don't think of myself as broken. I just **am**. I am the way I am, and the way I am is **exactly** the way I'm supposed to be. The flower taught me that."

"Oh, the flower! *You* know about the flower, too?!"

28

"Well, of course I do! You see, when I landed here on Crystal Pond, it wasn't just my wing that was broken. I was hurt on the inside, too. I hated myself because I was different and I was sure no one would ever love me the way I was. And then, I looked into the heart of the flower and saw myself the way I really am, *not* for who I am *not*. The flower showed me how to look at myself from the inside out, just like it showed you, and I learned that even though I might have a broken wing, *I* am not broken. I'm perfect just the way I am! And when I love myself, I am free to love everyone and everything else around me! That's when I start to feel really light. In fact, I feel *so* light, it's like I'm flying, indeed!"

"Oh, I know exactly what you mean!!" Daisy exclaimed. "When my mom died, I was mad at the world. And then I lost my leg and had to get a new one. At first, it felt *sooooo* heavy. It was hard to walk on and eveyone looked at me funny. I hated myself and all I wanted to do was run away, but I didn't think I could...you know, because of my leg. And then one day I just put one foot in front of the other and I took off! I ran and ran, and the more I ran, the lighter I got. It felt so good, I almost felt like *I* was flying, too! *And*...I was sure I heard my mother talking to me, too! Hmmm...it seems you and I have alot in common, don't we, Aldora?"

"Yes, dear. We certainly do. And Zara and Kaela, too. You see, *everything* on Crystal Pond used to be something else, yet nothing here is what it's supposed to be."

"Oh, I get it! I get it!! Thank you so much," Daisy shreiked, smiling as a gust of warm wind swirled overhead. For a moment, Daisy thought she felt her mother's hand brush against her face and when she looked back upon the shore, Aldora was gone.

Daisy stood facing Crystal Pond with her hands stretched high up to the sky as the trees were humming, the birds were chirping, and the warmth of the sun filled her heart. She listened closely as the wind whispered a deep secret in her ear. It told her,

"All the power you need is inside of you."

Daisy had no idea how long she'd been asleep, but she awoke to find herself lying on a bed of pine needles near the edge of the woods. She heard the familiar sound of children laughing and playing in the distance and followed the voices to Miss Judy's backyard.

"Jeepers, where did you run off to?" Jack asked when he saw Daisy coming. "You ran for those woods so fast, you gave Miss Judy a terrible fright! Don't tell her I said so," Jack leaned in and chuckled in her ear, "but it was kinda funny to watch. Anyway, I'm glad you're back," he continued. "Geez, I never saw anyone run so fast! Do you wanna be on my team, Daisy? C'mon...whatta ya say?"

Daisy looked at Jack and thought about it for a moment. Finally, she turned to him, shrugged her shoulders, and said, "sure, I guess so." Then, she did a cartwheel in the grass and smiled, landing safely on her own two feet.

"I AM THE WAY I AM
AND THE WAY I AM IS
EXACTLY THE WAY I'M
SUPPOSED TO BE."

—ALDORA, THE BUTTERFLY

I hope you've enjoyed your journey to Crystal Pond
with Daisy and her friends!

I've had a great time too, and I look forward
to sharing more of Daisy's adventures
with you in the future!

For additional information
or to join our mailing list, please contact:
www.lalefroisheath.com
e-mail: info@lalefroisheath.com

Thank you!

—Lisa A. LeFrois-Heath